Dance, Y'all, Dance

Kelly Bennett

illustrated by
Terri Murphy

Dance on!
Kelly Bennett

bright sky press
HOUSTON, TEXAS

bright sky press

2365 Rice Blvd., Suite 202 Houston, Texas 77005
www.brightskypress.com

ISBN 978-1-933979-65-6

10   9   8   7   6   5   4   3   2   1

Library of Congress information on file with publisher.

Book and cover design by Marla Garcia and Ellen Cregan
Illustrations by Terri Murphy
Printed in the United States of America

DEDICATION

For Ronnie, who helped me learn the steps.
This story lives because of you.

ACKNOWLEDGEMENTS

Pralines and big hugs to my sis-in-law Liz, who two-stepped
with me all the way home from San Antonio, and to my critique
buds, Marty, Varsha, Linda, Kathy, Laurie, Sydnie & Russell.

It's Saturday night. The Dance Hall's aglow.
Call Grams and our friends. Head to town for the show.

We worked hard all week. The chores are all done.
A country band's playin'. Let's join the fun.

Step-step, glide, glide,
Kick up your feet.
Dance, y'all, dance,
To a two-steppin' beat.

Here come the Browns with their twin baby girls.
Look! They have dimples and bright orange curls.

At a hundred 'n' two, Grand Pappy Skiddle
Is still slappin' spoons and bowin' his fiddle.

Step-step, glide, glide,
Stroll hand in hand.
Dance, y'all, dance,
Give a cheer for the band.

Ida Belle broke her left leg; Clint broke his right.
Won't keep them from swingin' this Saturday night.

"Please teach me to dance," Lil' Sister begs Pop.
Once Sis learns the steps, she won't want to stop.

Step-step, glide, glide,
Take a spin, y'all!
Do the Boot Scoot
'Round the Dance Hall.

When the band takes a break, folks slip outside.
"Crank it up, Henry! Let's go for a ride."

Buck's under the stage with Harlin and Beau.
They're up to no good—best let their folks know.

Step-step, glide, glide,
Cross arms and spin.
Slide up, swing 'round,
What a Pretzel you're in!

We hear a loud sneeze. Aunt May gives a shout:
"STOP DANCIN', Y'ALL! MY FALSE TEETH FLEW OUT!"

Music is playing, but Curt waits alone
While his dance partner talks on the new telephone.

Step-step, glide, glide,
Gents grab a girl.
Dance, y'all, dance,
Give your partner a twirl.

Amy Lou and Bubba are lookin' real glum.
They tried a new twirl and stepped in some gum.

Open the window. Hear that plane roar?
"Tip a wing, Lindy! Rev up and soar!"

Step-step, glide, glide,
Circle the floor.
When the song ends,
We all holler for more!

"Where's the band?" we ask. "They're dancin'," says Flo.
"The Opry is playin' on the new radio."

Jake stomps on Claire's toes and trips on her feet.
Claire doesn't mind 'cause Jake smiles so sweet.

Step-step, glide, glide,
Away we go!
Four turns, fast hands,
Now that's Pistachio!

Sallie and Jem traded "I dos" today.
One dance for luck, then he'll whisk her away.

Rosie peeks at Will. He gives her a wink.
"You like him?" we ask. Rose blushes bright pink.

Step-step, glide, glide,
Gals, close your eyes.
Dance, y'all, dance,
It's a Sweetheart Surprise.

The last song is done. Head out to the truck.
Call Grams. Catch the twins and whistle for Buck.

Wave 'bye to our friends. "So long and sleep tight.
See y'all at the Dance Hall, next Saturday night."

AUTHOR'S NOTE

Was a time in small town America when, on most every weekend night, folks gathered at dance halls. Some folks came to hear the music—many of the finest Country and Western bands got their start playing and singing in dance halls. Some folks came to catch up on the news, talk about the weather, farming, business, and politics. Some came to visit with neighbors and friends. Everyone—young and old, rich and poor, short, tall, long-haired, or bald—came to tap their toes, clap their hands and dance!

Dance halls got their start in the early days of the western movement. Settlers, used to the bustling liveliness of the cities back East, found carving a life on the prairie to be hard and lonely. Back then, there were no radios, televisions, or telephones bringing folks information or entertainment. There were no computers—no e-mail, either—and mail delivery was slow at best. After a busy week spent tending their farms, building fences, caring for livestock, hoeing, planting, and harvesting crops, settlers looked forward to their weekly trip into town. When their shopping was done, they headed to the dance hall. The dance hall was much more than just a place to dance: it was where neighbors and friends gathered to visit, swap stories, celebrate, share hardship, and laugh.

Still today, folks all over America gather in dance halls to listen to music and dance. One of the oldest, continuously operating dance halls is in Gruene, Texas, a small town located in the Texas Hill Country between Austin and San Antonio. Gruene Hall (pronounced Green) was built in 1878. Once the music starts, Gruene's scarred walls and smooth, wooden-plank floors ring with the sound of guitars, fiddles, and drums pounding out Country and Western tunes. Couples dressed in tight jeans, pearl-buttoned shirts, boots, and cowboy hats circle the floor, two-stepping to the familiar six-count beat.

The Two-Step, or Texas Two-Step, is the most well-known Country and Western dance. The boy and girl face each other and clasp hands. The boy holds his partner's waist with his right hand. The girl rests her left hand on her partner's shoulder. The basic Two-Step is very simple, consisting of four steps to a six-count beat. Two short, quick steps followed by two longer, two-count steps: Step-step, gli—de, gli—de; step-step, gli—de, gli—de. Dancing couples circle the floor in a counter-clockwise direction, with the boys facing forward and the girls moving backwards, two-stepping and twirling in time with the music.

A more advanced form of the Two-Step is called Western Swing. Turns, hand movements, and variations with names such as Sweetheart Surprise, Pretzel, Side Travel, Wild West Shuffle, Conversation, and Pistachio are added to the basic step.

Now, come on, y'all! Scrub up, dress up, and…dance, y'all, dance!